Four Puppies

By ANNE HEATHERS

Pictures by LILIAN OBLIGADO

A GOLDEN BOOK · NEW YORK
Western Publishing Company, Inc.
Racine, Wisconsin 53404

There were once four new puppies who lived in a warm dark corner by the stove. Those puppies had never been outdoors because they were too little.

They didn't know about sky or trees or grass.

They didn't even know about Summer or Fall or Winter or Spring UNTIL . . .

. . . they were old enough to go out the door to the sunny porch outside.

At first the stairs were too big for the little puppies to go down. Then one day the stairs didn't look so big any more.

"They are smaller," said one puppy.

"No—we are bigger," said his brothers.

Then those four little puppies went flop, hop, and tumble, down the stairs and into the great big world outside.

They sniffed the fresh green smell of the grass.

They raced on the grass and they rolled on the grass and they turned somersaults in the grass all afternoon.

"Oh my—what a fine place this is," said the four little puppies.

Every day the four puppies went out to play.

They pounced at caterpillars.

They chased butterflies.

They ran round and round after their shadows.

They had so much fun that they hated to go inside—even when there was nice, hot chicken broth for supper!

Then one morning the stairs looked even smaller.

"And we're even bigger!" said the puppies.

And they walked down those stairs—plop! plop! plop!—as easy as pie.

But the four little puppies were so busy playing that they didn't see that the big world was changing too UNTIL . . .

. . . it had changed so much that they couldn't play the same games any more.

A funny little wind tickled their ears. They didn't have shadows because the sun was behind a cloud. The grass felt cool. The butterflies had gone. The caterpillars were hiding.

And the leaves began to turn yellow and red.

"Oh dear," said the puzzled puppies.

The next day—whoosh!—the wind knocked all the petals off a rose.

And—swoosh!—it blew the leaves right off the trees.

Those four puppies tried to put the petals back on the rose.

They tried to put the leaves back on the trees.

But they couldn't, so they started to cry.

"You silly-billies—there's nothing to cry about," said a friendly red squirrel in the hickory tree.

"When the leaves turn red and yellow and come off the trees it means that SUMMER is over and FALL has come. Why, you'll just have more fun than ever!"

And the squirrel was right.

Leaves as crisp as cornflakes covered the ground.

The four little puppies scuffed around in leaves and buried themselves under leaves and kicked leaves up in the air.

They had so much fun that they hated to go inside — even when there were lamb chops for supper!

Then one morning when the puppies went out to play they didn't have to walk — plop! plop! — down the stairs. They could jump down the steps two at a time.

"They are even smaller," said one puppy.

"No—we are even bigger," said his brothers.

But they didn't see that the big world was changing too UNTIL...

. . . it had changed so much that they couldn't play the same games any more. The water in the puddles was as hard as glass. A rough wind blew their ears back, and blew the leaves clear out of the yard.

"Oh dear," cried the puzzled little puppies.
They tried to hold onto the leaves, but still they
blew away, faster and faster.
So the puppies started to cry.

"You silly-billies—there's nothing to cry about,"
said the friendly red squirrel in the hickory tree.
"When there's ice on the puddles and the North
Wind blows it means that Fall is over and Winter
has come. You'll just have more fun than ever!"

And the squirrel was right—for the next day when the puppies went out to play, everything was white with snow!

Every day after that those four little puppies parted snow with their noses and slid down the bank and made footprints in the snow.

They had so much fun that they hated to go inside—even when there were great big beef bones for supper!

One morning the puppies were so big they could jump down the stairs three at a time.

But they didn't notice that the big world was changing too UNTIL...

...it had changed so much that they couldn't play the same games any more.

The sunshine was warmer. It wasn't raining, but the water kept drip-dripping from the trees. The snow bank was too small to slide down.

And the next day there were bare brown patches of ground with no snow at all!

"Oh dear," cried the puzzled little puppies. They tried to push the snow into a pile so they could keep it to play with. But the snow turned to water and sank into the ground right under their paws. So the puppies started to cry.

"You silly-billies—there's nothing to cry about," said the friendly red squirrel in the hickory tree.

"When the sun gets warmer and melts the snow it means that WINTER is over and SPRING has come—and you'll soon guess for yourselves what comes after Spring. It's like a wheel turning round and round."

And the squirrel was right.

Some tiny green stalks poked up out of the ground. The puppies and the stalks grew bigger every day. And one day the puppies jumped down all the steps at once and found leaves and flowers on every stalk.

"That's how the big world looked when we first saw it!" they cried.

And they began to bark happily, for they had guessed what comes after Spring.

"SUMMER is what comes after Spring!" cried the first puppy. "Butterflies again!"

"Then Fall," said the second puppy. "Crisp leaves again!"

"Then Winter," said the third puppy. "Nice white snow again!"

"Then Spring," said the fourth puppy. "Brand-new leaves again!"

"AND EVERYTHING STARTS ALL OVER AGAIN EVERY SPRING!" all the puppies cried together.

The friendly red squirrel looked down at them from the hickory tree.

"Now that you know all that, you are not puzzled little puppies any more," he said.

"What are we then?" asked the puppies.

"You are big brave dogs," he said.

And the squirrel was right— as usual.